Marshmallow Pie the Cat Superstar *in Hollywood*

## Books by Clara Vulliamy

MARSHMALLOW PIE THE CAT SUPERSTAR

MARSHMALLOW PIE THE CAT SUPERSTAR: ON TV

MARSHMALLOW PIE THE CAT SUPERSTAR: IN HOLLYWOOD

*The Dotty Detective series
in reading order*

DOTTY DETECTIVE

THE PAW PRINT PUZZLE

THE MIDNIGHT MYSTERY

THE LOST PUPPY

THE BIRTHDAY SURPRISE

THE HOLIDAY MYSTERY

# Marshmallow Pie the Cat Superstar *in Hollywood*

## Clara Vulliamy

HarperCollins *Children's Books*

First published in Great Britain by
HarperCollins *Children's Books* in 2020
HarperCollins *Children's Books* is a division of HarperCollins*Publishers* Ltd
1 London Bridge Street
London SE1 9GF

www.harpercollins.co.uk

HarperCollins*Publishers*
1st Floor, Watermarque Building, Ringsend Road
Dublin 4, Ireland

1

ISBN 978-0-00-846136-2

Clara Vulliamy asserts the moral right to be identified as the author
and illustrator of the work.
A CIP catalogue record for this title is available from the British Library.

Printed and bound in the UK using 100% renewable electricity
at CPI Group (UK) Ltd

*For Julia, with much love*

# Map of the hotel suite

HUGE bathroom

Fancy shampoos and bubble baths

Amelia's bedroom

↑ ↑ ↑
Amazing views of Hollywood

(I hate baths)

Fancy sofa and chair

Amazing views of the snacks

↙ ↙ ↙

Biggest bed EVER

Shower ↓

Robe and slippers for Amelia

My bed is a pile of fancy cushions on a soft fluffy rug

Every day TWO CHOCOLATES are left on Amelia's pillow!

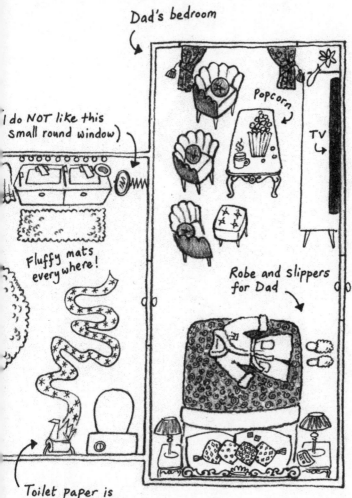

Dad's bedroom

I do NOT like this small round window!

Popcorn

TV

Fluffy mats every where!

Robe and slippers for Dad

Toilet paper is folded into a swan shape, and covered in stars

# Chapter One
## Hello, Hollywood!

My name is Marshmallow Pie and I am an INTERNATIONAL SUPERSTAR.

Here we are, arriving in Hollywood: me, my human—*Amelia Lime*—and her dad. I have been cast in a major new movie, playing the very important role of the villain's cat. I got the part when a famous producer saw a video of me that became very popular online.

He could see *immediately* that I was HUGELY talented—and feisty!

We are met off the plane by a chauffeur wearing mirrored sunglasses and holding up a sign.

MARSHMALLOW PIE
AMELIA LIME
MR. LIME

He picks up our suitcases and we follow him to a gleaming white stretch limousine.

"This is AMAZING!" says Amelia
happily, trying out the buttons that
control the multicolored lighting.

"Not bad!" agrees her dad, sinking back
into the plump leather seats.

It IS very luxurious, even for a cat of my
importance.

As we are driven smoothly towards
the city, Amelia gazes out of the window
in wonder.

We've never been to America before, or any faraway places. "It's all so different," she says, "and SO exciting!"

I concentrate on exploring the snack compartments. A large packet of **Cod Crispies** has been thoughtfully provided; it would be rude not to eat them all.

We soon arrive at our hotel. As we cross the shiny marble floor of the lobby, dodging between the wealthy-

looking guests, I am dazzled for a moment by the lights of the *massive* chandelier above.

We check in and
go to the elevator,
which is operated
by a very fancy
bellboy. I love his
bright red jacket
with gold buttons
and matching hat. I
would look *fantastic*
in an outfit like that.
When we reach our
floor, I stiffen my
legs and refuse to
come out, insisting
that we go up and
down several more
times, until Amelia
says, "I think that's
enough now, Pie."

Our suite is VERY grand. I share a bedroom with Amelia, her dad has another, and there's a bathroom joining our rooms together.

Amelia throws herself down onto the **HUGE** bed. "I've NEVER seen so many pillows and cushions in my whole life!" she says.

Her dad looks around and whistles.

"You could practically fit our whole apartment into just this bathroom!"

I **STRETCH** out on a soft, furry white rug. It is *almost* as fluffy as me.

Amelia unpacks our things and arranges some of the cushions on the floor to make a little bed for me next to hers. We look out of the window at the busy city, all lit up as it begins to get dark.

"I can't believe we're really here," says Amelia. "It's like a *dream!* And it's all thanks to your talent, Pie."

But I take it all in my stride. The
GLITZ, the *glamour*, the
luxury . . . I feel completely at home.

"And now I think we should get an early
night," says her dad, yawning. "We've
had a VERY long day, and we've got a
big meeting about the movie first thing
tomorrow morning."

# Chapter Two
## Coolest on the Catwalk

After breakfast we go down to the lobby to meet Dexter, my agent from the Ace Animal Acting Agency. He will come to the meeting with us.

"Hey, guys, great to see you all!" he says. "Looking good, Pie!"

I am wearing the green bow tie Amelia made for me. She says it's important to make a good first impression.

We follow Dexter into the hotel conference room, where all the major people from the movie are gathered.

"Oh dear, I feel very nervous," says Amelia, hesitating in the doorway. "This is such a BIG moment for Pie!"

"Don't worry," says her dad. "Everyone is going to love him!"

*That's true,* I think to myself. *Of course they will! They've all seen my video.* Dexter introduces us to everyone. There are too many people to remember, but a few catch my attention.

There's the big Hollywood producer, Rocky Milan, striding up and down and giving orders to his assistant, who hurries along behind and writes things in a notebook. . . .

1. Vacuum red carpet
2. Order 10 crates of champagne
3. Polish villain's black swivel chair
4. Pick up cat jewelry
5. Hire sharks

HIRE ME

CV

There's the actress who will play the role of the villain, the glamorous *Tallulah Lush*, drinking coffee, her face half-hidden by a huge hat and sunglasses . . .

And then there's Tallulah's daughter, Madison.

"Madison is a professional model, a big name in her own right," whispers Dexter. "She also sells products with her famous catchphrase written on them. That's it there, on her T-shirt—GOOLEST ON THE GATWALK."

Then he says more loudly, "Madison, this is Amelia. She's only a couple of years younger than you—I'm sure you're going to be *GREAT* friends!"

Madison looks up from her phone, but she barely glances at Amelia. Instead, her eyes light up when she sees me. She gives me the brightest, whitest smile.

"Marshmallow Pie!" exclaims Madison in a charming accent. "It's AWESOME to meet you at last! Your video is *amazing*! Everyone's talking about you."

I'm *very* flattered. I look at Madison's catchphrase, written in sparkly pink gemstones:

## COOLEST ON THE CATWALK

It could have been made for me! I notice her **BIG** hair, so similar to my fluffy fur. And what's more, she's a superstar, just like me.

We are *so* alike.

Amelia looks shy, glancing down at her jeans and plain sweater. "Yes, I'm really proud of him," she says.

While Amelia's dad talks with the other adults and fills in some forms, we sit down with Madison and she tells us all about herself.

"*Everywhere* I go," she sighs, "I'm approached by reporters and fans.

At the beach, having my hair done, eating at restaurants,

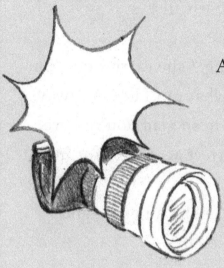

I'm *always* asked to pose for photos and sign autographs."

I understand completely. It's one of the many burdens of being a huge celebrity. (Well, okay, it hasn't happened to me yet, but I'm sure it will.)

"It's SO annoying," she carries on, "but I'm famous, so what can I do? Anyway, Marshmallow, I'm so glad you're here. You'll be the perfect accessory for me."

"It's Pie," says Amelia quietly, "and 'accessory' isn't really—"

But Madison just carries on. "So I've decided: whenever you aren't busy filming, I'll show you around town. We'll start straight away. As soon as this *boring* meeting is finished, I'm taking you SHOPPING!"

I purr happily. It's going to be
*AMAZING*, hanging out with
Madison.

# Chapter Three
## Meowdy!

Madison has her own car, a fast little pink convertible, even though she's too young to drive herself. We all squeeze in—the driver, me, Amelia, Madison, and her bodyguard, Big Barbara.

Her driver takes us along the grandest
streets, with crowds bustling in and out
of fancy clothes shops. Then he pulls up
outside PAW-JAMAS, a very expensive-
looking pet boutique.

"Did you tell the press we were coming?" asks Amelia, noticing a cluster of photographers waiting outside. "I thought you said you find them annoying. . . ."

But Madison doesn't seem to hear her. She just beams and waves as we all get out of the car. Then she lifts me out of Amelia's arms and holds me up so the

photographers can take lots of pictures
of us together.

"This is Marshmallow Pie!" she tells
them. "The internet sensation. I'm sure
you recognize him!"

I smile blissfully for the cameras. It's so
kind of Madison to say I'm a sensation.

She waves one more time, then we turn and head into the shop.

The PAW-JAMAS staff are SO friendly to Madison.

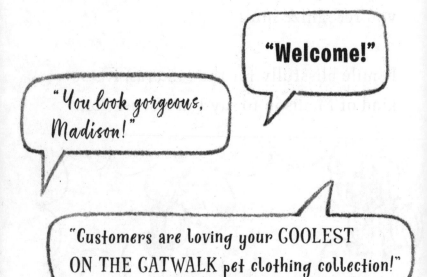

"Welcome!"

"You look gorgeous, Madison!"

"Customers are loving your COOLEST ON THE CATWALK pet clothing collection!"

I am IMPRESSED. This is how we celebrities like to be greeted.

I try on loads of fabulous outfits. We are there for HOURS, while Big Barbara watches from a distance, looking bored.

Amelia tries to help, but Madison has very clear ideas about what would suit me best.

# Coolest Cat on the Catwalk!

Madison selects a pink, sparkly COOLEST ON THE CATWALK bandana and Stetson, to match her T-shirt. She obviously knows a lot about how a star should dress. I am pleased that we now look even more alike.

"Oh my, what a cute cowboy!" Madison chirps, posing for a selfie with me. "Howdy, Pie—or should I say, 'Meowdy'?" The shop assistants all laugh.

Then Madison turns her attention to my green bow tie.

"Time to replace this old thing," she says, taking it off and casually tossing it to Amelia.

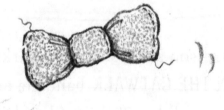

Madison then picks up a shiny gold satin bow tie and puts it on me. "There!" she says. "SO much better! Your old one looked kinda homemade. REAL stars wear chic accessories from stores like this."

I admire my new gold bow tie in the mirror. It's **very snazzy.** I still love my green bow tie, though. I'm sure Madison didn't mean to be rude. She probably didn't realize that it was Amelia who made it for me.

45

When we finally get back to our hotel, Amelia's dad is waiting for us with delicious-smelling pizza slices wrapped up in **crinkly** paper. There is a little extra salami for me, as a treat.

At bedtime, while Amelia is brushing her teeth in the vast bathroom, I investigate the interesting toilet paper. The end is folded into the shape of a

swan, and when I
manage to undo it
I find the entire roll
is covered in tiny
silver stars.

I unroll lots and lots of it,

to really appreciate the effect.

"You are one **crazy** cat, Pie!"
Amelia says, and she laughs. She
seems more cheerful again now.
"I hope you'll be on your BEST
behavior when you start filming
tomorrow!"

I settle down for the night, feeling good, ready for *sweet dreams* about gold bow ties, and adoring photographers, and as much salami as I can eat.

I *LOVE* Hollywood!

# Chapter Four

## Back in the Spotlight

"Ready for your first day's filming?"
Amelia asks me the next morning.

Ready for

the CAMERAS,

the BRIGHT LIGHTS,

the ACTION?

## YOU BET I AM!

"The film studio is sending a car straight after breakfast," says her dad, "so we'd better get a move on."

Amelia smiles. "It will be good to get started. You're going to be brilliant, Pie!"

Yes. I am brilliant. I perform my role perfectly—everybody says so. I look especially marvelous in a diamond collar.

All I have to do is sit on the villain's lap while she spins around on a black swivel chair to face the camera, stroking the top of my head. The telephone rings and she answers it, saying,

## "RELEASE THE SNAKES!"

HA

Then she gives an evil laugh, and I smile my meanest, most sinister smile.

HA

HA

HA

HA

HA

HA

# Acting Superstar

Later, to celebrate a very successful first day's filming, Amelia's dad takes us to the hotel's fancy roof terrace restaurant for dinner.

"I've never been *anywhere* like this before," says Amelia, wide-eyed, looking around at the sumptuous decorations,

the colorful umbrellas, and the views of the distant mountains. "LOOK!" she exclaims. "The famous Hollywood sign!"

We sit down next to a potted palm tree while waiters hurry past, holding up trays laden with amazing delicacies.

While Amelia and her dad wait for their food to arrive, they chat about the filming and what fun it was.

"*Tallulah Lush* is really scary as the villain," says Amelia.

"She's quite a character," agrees her dad. "Her evil laugh made my hair stand on end!"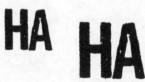

Amelia giggles, but then she looks over my head towards the door and I see her spirits sink a little. I don't know why, because a moment later Madison sweeps up to our table.

I'm SO pleased to see her.

She pulls up a chair and takes out her phone. "Check this out!" she says, showing us a picture on her social media app. It's the photograph of her posing with me in PAW-JAMAS pet boutique the day before.

"My fans *ADORE* Pie. It's already got *loads* of likes!" she tells us.

I'm not surprised. We look stunning together.

Then Madison carries on, "Did you know they do an *amazing* pets' menu here?" and she loudly summons a waiter.

## I CANNOT BELIEVE MY EYES.

In no time at all, dish after dish of mouth-watering food is being delivered to our table—all for me!

"Go on, try everything!" encourages Madison.

"Pie usually only has one meal a day," says Amelia, looking worried, "with just an *occasional* treat. All this food . . . it's too rich for him."

"Oh, don't be a killjoy!" says Madison. "Anyway, fat cats are SO cute and funny. He'd get EVEN MORE likes online if he put on a little weight!"

I don't know about that, but I do know
that I like the look of the **SALMON
MOUSSE SUNDAE** that's just arrived.

It's all abuzz because now Dexter arrives
too, hurrying over in a state of huge
EXCITEMENT.

"I hoped I'd find you here," he says. "I have news. There might—might—be a chance of an interview for Pie and Amelia with **VANITY FUR.** It's America's TOP fashionable pets' magazine!"

"Wow!" says Amelia.

"Well done, you guys!" says Madison. "That would be *wild!*"

"Fingers crossed!" says Dexter.

Madison narrows her eyes as if considering something, and then starts texting.

Meanwhile Dexter shows us copies of **VANITY FUR.**

They all feature only the *finest* animal stars. I would fit right in! I hope they agree to write about me.

VANITY FUR

EXCLUSIVE! At home with Lord Alfonso

NITY FUR

TWINKLE TOES WINS AN OSCAR!

VANITY FUR

VANITY FUR

VANITY FUR

*Lovely Louella steals the heart of the nation!*

I notice that Amelia takes this opportunity to move the dishes of rich food out of my reach. This makes me cross. I could have managed a *few* more mouthfuls. I'm sure Madison would have let me finish.

When we get back to our room, Amelia hangs up her dress with a sigh and gets ready for bed. I just collapse heavily on my mound of cushions.

Amelia climbs under the covers and shuts her eyes.

But soon she opens them again because I
meow VERY LOUDLY.

I have a **TERRIBLE** stomach ache.

# Chapter Five
## Puffed Up and Perfect

Amelia is a bit tired the next morning.
"I was awake worrying about you, Pie,"
she says, "after you ate all that rich food
and felt so sick!"

But I am FINE again
now. I wander into the
bathroom, where I get
an unpleasant surprise.
There seems to be a
small, round window in
here, with an alarmingly
HUGE cat peering in. I try not
to catch his eye and hurry out again.

After breakfast we head back to the studio for another morning of filming.

In today's scene the villain stands at a window, holding me and looking out over the city, saying, "One day all of this will be mine, I tell you—*all mine. . . .*"

Then I **purr** and look out of the window too, with a menacing expression.

● REC

00:00:00

Again, everything goes brilliantly. I'm taking to Hollywood like a duck to water.

And now it's time for more FUN with Madison. I cannot wait.

Her car pulls up outside the studio and her driver toots the horn. Madison waves and opens the door. I hurry over and jump up onto the seat next to her. Amelia follows slowly behind.

"I have an *amazing* treat booked for you, Pie," announces Madison. "I'm taking you to the

💙
Happy Tails
**PET SPA!**"

I have never been to a spa before. It's obviously the kind of thing celebrities like me should do a LOT, so I am very glad to have Madison as my guide.

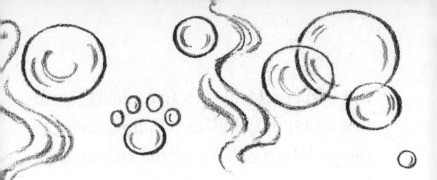

When we arrive at *Happy Tails* **PET SPA**, it's the smell that hits us first. Clouds of perfume and fur-spray come wafting towards us. Amelia immediately starts coughing. We peer through a haze of steam and bubbles, and I see that the spa is already full of many different pets, who are being shampooed and styled, having a pedicure, or relaxing in the Jacuzzi.

Big Barbara, Madison's fierce bodyguard, looks a bit out of place standing among the pink fluffy cushions and ribbons and bows.

## Guests at the Pet Spa

Before I'm handed over to the staff
for my treatments, Madison takes a
hairbrush out of her bag with a flourish
and begins brushing my fur herself. She
asks Amelia to take photos.

Madison's hairbrush, like her T-shirt,
has COOLEST ON THE CATWALK
written on it in sparkly pink lettering.

"And now," Madison proposes, "let's try out the perfumes! I'm just the right person to choose the perfect fragrance for you, Pie."

Amelia tries to join in. "Pie likes napping in our laundry basket, so how about *Fresh Linen?*" she suggests. "Or this one—*Meadow Lawn*. Pie loves to roll in the grass!"

But Madison doesn't seem to hear her and chooses Intense Cinnamon and Rose. Amelia starts coughing again. To be honest it IS a little overpowering.

Then I have my treatments. My fur is in curlers, my whiskers are combed, and my paws are moisturized with catnip-scented cream. *Bliss!*

"Some owners don't really have an eye for *glamour*," Madison says to the spa therapist, glancing down at Amelia's bitten nails, then back at her own glittery manicure. "So it's lucky Pie has me now!"

One more spray of perfume, one more photograph, and it's time to leave.

Amelia is quiet on the way back to the hotel, but I am utterly *entranced* by my fabulous reflection in the car window. I have been backcombed and floofed-up so much I am *twice* my normal size.

I might feel a little bit itchy from all the products, but I look

SPECTACULAR.

# Chapter Six
## Putting the ME in Meow

The next morning, when we walk out of the hotel to wait for our lift to the studio, we are surprised to see a handful of fans gathered outside . . . waiting for ME!

"Hey! Marshmallow Pie! Can we get a photo?" they call out, leaning in to take selfies with me.

"You're becoming famous, Pie," says
Amelia, once we're in the car. She smiles
at me, although she seems a bit startled
too. "I suppose those photos the press
took of you and Madison must be on all
the celebrity news websites by now."

"Not to mention he's all over Madison's social media again," says her dad. "Look!"

He shows us on his phone.

❤ 12,321

**Madison Lush**
Glamour puss Marshmallow Pie LOVES my #CoolestOnTheCatwalk hairbrush! Another PURRFECT day together.

There are pictures of Madison and me at the *Happy Tails* **PET SPA** all smiles, her sparkly hairbrush catching the light.

I see that Amelia is biting her nails, something she only does when she's anxious. "I suppose it's helping Pie get the attention he deserves," she says, ". . . but I can't help feeling Madison cares more about selling her things than about Pie."

I don't know what Amelia is talking about. This is the life! I'm FAMOUS, and *everybody* wants to be my friend.

Things are great at the studio too. In the scene we are filming today, the villain jumps to her feet, picks me up, shouts "PREPARE MY PRIVATE JET FOR TAKE-OFF!", and strides out of the room.

I give a fierce yowl, and my diamond collar twinkles and shines. I am magnificent.

But Amelia is a bit quiet. Her dad looks at her. "This is all very tiring," he says. "After the filming's over for today, let's have a restful afternoon back at the hotel."

Amelia is lying on her bed reading a book, while I settle down for a catnap. Her dad has a cup of tea and is watching a police drama on TV. On the screen are two mean-looking crooks. One of them has a grouchy dog. . . .

"Hang on a minute," exclaims Amelia, just as my eyes have closed. "That dog—it's *Buster*!"

I open my eyes. UNBELIEVABLE. It *is* him.

Buster lives in the apartment below us at home. He is an actor too. To be honest, I've never forgiven him for ruining my first ever audition. Plus, whenever I get a new chance to shine, he seems to catch a lucky break as well.

Now here he is, in Hollywood, like me. It's SO annoying. We just can't get away from him.

I soon cheer up, though, because Dexter phones Amelia with some *EXCELLENT* NEWS. . . .

"We've got it—the **VANITY FUR** interview for you and Pie!" he tells her. "And it's happening tomorrow!"

# *"AMAZING!"* replies Amelia.

"There's one condition, though," Dexter carries on. "They want Pie to do a *very special* photoshoot with Madison afterwards."

"Oh," says Amelia.

For a moment I think that Amelia doesn't look very happy as she hangs up the phone, but I must be mistaken because she puts on her best, most cheerful smile.

"I'm so happy for you, Pie!" she says to me. "I'll be really proud to do the interview with you, and I'm sure the photoshoot will be fantastic too."

A little later, I hear Amelia and her dad chatting together. "When Madison heard about the interview the other night," Amelia says, "I saw her busy texting someone. She might have suggested the photoshoot to **VANITY FUR** then."

"I wouldn't be surprised," agrees her dad. "She certainly seems to know everyone in town."

You'd think today couldn't get any better, but then there's a knock on the door. The bellboy delivers a package, and it's for **ME.**

Inside is a hamper of gifts. There's a shiny satin pillow, a packet of fishy snacks, and a cat-sized baseball cap—all emblazoned with the COOLEST ON THE CATWALK logo.

There's a note inside too. It says:

Madison Lush

Wear this hat to
your interview,
Pie—you'll look
INCREDIBLE!

Madison xoxo

I am thrilled with my presents. Madison is SO generous.

I squeeze into the now-empty hamper, cleaning a few fishy crumbs from my whiskers and enjoying the rustle of the gold tissue paper.

I LOVE this trip more and more each day. My first ever fans approached me this morning, I have an interview with **VANITY FUR** tomorrow, AND I have fancy gifts to enjoy—all thanks to Madison. I am SO lucky to have found my new friend.

# ⌃ ⌃
# ≡Chapter Seven≡
## Best Friends Forever

The next morning, Amelia, her dad,
and I arrive for our interview at the
**VANITY FUR** offices. I am wearing
my COOLEST ON THE CATWALK
baseball cap, just as Madison asked
me to.

"I'm really pleased we can do this interview together, Pie," says Amelia. "I'm so proud of how far you've come."

I feel happy too. It doesn't seem long ago that Amelia was training me for my first audition, and now I'm a Hollywood star! I suddenly feel very grateful that she's always had faith in me, and I give her a little nuzzle.

Dexter is waiting for us inside. We leave Amelia's dad in reception, flicking through the magazines, and follow Dexter to a very snazzy office.

All the furniture is gleaming silver, and the walls are covered in signed photographs of celebrity pets.

Madison is here already, chatting and laughing with the journalist, even though the photoshoot isn't until afterwards.

As soon as we are seated, the journalist turns to us with a friendly smile. "So, Amelia and Pie, how are you enjoying your visit to Hollywood?"

COOLEST
ON THE
CATWALK

"Oh, Pie is LOVING Hollywood!" Madison answers for us. "I've taken him to all the *coolest* places. We've been having so much fun!"

Madison is right, but this is meant to be *Amelia's* big moment. Amelia struggles to make herself heard because Madison keeps jumping in to answer the questions.

"And how did Pie get started with his acting career?" the journalist asks us.

"Well—" 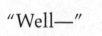 Amelia begins, her eyes brightening.

"I taught him everything he knows!"

Madison interrupts.

"I coached him. You might say I made him into a star!"

*That's not strictly true*, I think to myself. I begin to feel uneasy. Why is

Madison saying this? I would never be here if it wasn't for Amelia.

"Pie has risen from unknown animal actor to video sensation to movie star," the journalist continues. "What do you feel has led to his success?"

"Pie is awesome," Madison replies, "but I'd say his success is all down to the support of his *favorite* person. . . ."

I glance over at Amelia in relief. NOW she's going to get her big acknowledgement!

"And that's ME, of course," Madison declares with a little laugh. "I am Marshmallow Pie's BEST FRIEND."

Oh no. This time there is no mistaking it. Amelia looks sad and hurt, and I am sure I see tears in her eyes.

# THIS ISN'T RIGHT.

But there's no time to fix it, because the journalist is getting to her feet.

"We're running late. Time to head over to the photoshoot," she announces. "We're going to the Forecourt of the Stars! This is where the most famous Hollywood celebrities are invited to leave their handprints in the cement on the sidewalk. We've arranged for Pie to add his pawprints, and Madison will help him!"

"This is a GREAT honor, Pie!" says Dexter.

"Thanks to ME!" adds Madison. "Come on, let's go!"

She grabs me and marches back through reception, with Amelia and the others hurrying along behind. Amelia's dad jumps to his feet and follows too.

I JIGGLE and BOUNCE in Madison's arms as we rush on ahead down the street.

And it starts to dawn on me . . .

I have been dazzled by Madison. I thought she was so kind and generous, showing me exciting places, taking photos with me, and giving me presents.

But was it ever *really* about me? Or was she just trying to get more attention for herself all along, like Amelia said?

I think back to everything my human has done for me, right from the very start. It was AMELIA who trained me and started my career, but that's not all.

She looks after me, worries about me, and understands me best. She loves me, not for what *she* can get, but for myself.

She doesn't push to the front and show off, or wear expensive clothes and have her nails done, but Amelia is perfect, just as she is.

We make a great team, me and Amelia. *She* is my best friend.

By the time we arrive at the Forecourt of the Stars, a large crowd has gathered and the photographers are waiting. In a cordoned-off area, a square of wet cement has been specially prepared for my pawprints.

"Here he comes!" the photoshoot director announces through a megaphone. "*It's* MARSHMALLOW PIE!"

An excited hubbub rises from the crowd.

"Look this way, Madison!" call out the photographers.

Madison begins lowering me into the cement.

But this is **ALL WRONG**— I don't want to do this.

I glimpse Amelia making her way to the front of the crowd, and I twist and turn frantically to escape.

"He's trying to get away!" Madison cries out, gripping me tightly.

At last I wriggle free and leap from Madison's arms!

The COOLEST ON THE CATWALK baseball cap falls off and rolls away . . .

. . . and as I land and make a dash for Amelia, my back paws flick wet cement all over Madison's pink gemstone-encrusted tracksuit. I knock into the barrier too, sending three steel posts crashing noisily to the ground.

"My outfit!" cries Madison.

I jump up into Amelia's arms and *purr* loudly. *This* is where I belong.

"Look at them! This is just adorable!" the director calls out. "Is that Amelia, Pie's owner? Hey, Pie, Amelia—come and finish the photoshoot!"

So it's Amelia who gently helps me to make my pawprints in the cement. This time it's Madison in the background. She is sulking, making a fuss about her dirty clothes.

Amelia smiles happily, the cameras flash, and the crowd erupts into cheers and applause.

"I don't usually like having my photograph taken," Amelia says to her dad as we stroll back to our hotel. "But this time I can't wait to show everyone at home!"

"I've had a word with the journalist who did the interview," Dexter tells us, "as I'm not entirely sure she was given the right information. The magazine has agreed to ask you some more questions, *without* Madison there this time."

It turns out **VANITY FUR** has a title for the article. It will be . . .

# Chapter Eight
## Time to Go Home

A few days go past.

Amelia finishes the new interview, and I finish my filming—which involves doing the same scenes many more times but from a *slightly* different angle. The producer, Rocky Milan, says we are free to go. The film won't be released until later in the year, but it promises to be a **HUGE** hit.

We haven't seen or heard from Madison since the day of the photoshoot, but I don't mind. I know now she wasn't a real friend after all. Everything is much calmer and more relaxing now.

"We're better off without people like that in our life, Pie," Amelia says. "But I hope that Madison has learned something important. She needs to think of others if she's ever going to have a real friendship like ours."

It's our last night in Hollywood. We are in our hotel room, bags packed.

Dad has his feet up, reading the newspaper. I am sitting on Amelia's lap, purring contentedly.

"What would you like to do on our last evening here?" Amelia asks me. "We have so much to celebrate—your fantastic movie success especially!"

It's true. Although things with Madison turned out badly, I have a *stunning* career on the big screen to celebrate. *But there are more important things than that*, I think to myself, moving in closer for a cuddle.

Amelia gently brushes my fur. "That's the last of the backcombing and sticky fur-spray from the pet spa gone," she laughs, putting my green bow tie back on. "You look normal again!"

Luckily, my "normal" look is amazing enough as it is.

"What shall we do for dinner?" asks Amelia's dad. "Shall we go back to the roof terrace restaurant?"

"No," says Amelia. "Let's just be cozy together here and watch a movie with some popcorn."

So that's what we do.

It certainly has been an amazing trip.
But I realize I am looking forward
to going home too. Because even an
international superstar like me needs a
break from the high life. *Sometimes.*

# The End